OPEN VEINS

Ria Gupta

BlueRoseONE.com
Stories Matter
NewDelhi • London

BLUEROSE PUBLISHERS
India | U.K.

BlueRose ONE.com
Stories Matter
NewDelhi • London

For permissions requests or inquiries regarding this publication, please contact:

BLUEROSE PUBLISHERS
www.BlueRoseONE.com
info@bluerosepublishers.com
+91 8882 898 898
+4407342408967

ISBN: 978-93-7310-914-5

Cover design: Yash Singhal
Typesetting: Namrata Saini

First Edition: December 2025

"To all
Who have suffered in silence,
You are not alone."

Acknowledgements

“Open Veins” is my first book and is very close to me. Each word has been woven by the core of my heart.

I would like to extend my gratitude to those who’ve always supported me.

I hope this book reaches everyone who felt that they were alone. No matter what you are going through, you, yourself, will always be there for you. This book is for you.

Section 1

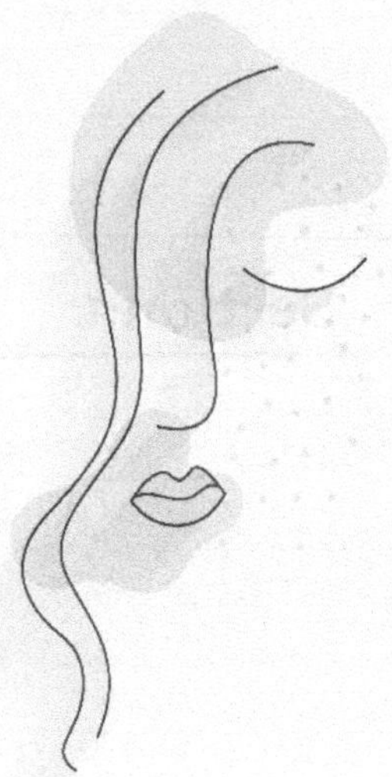

She loved shiny things; so bright,
Things that had spark delighted her.
Stars and moon were her favourites,
She saw the sun shining through the waves;
And in the end, after all,
She faded into the sparks - once and for all.

The way my thoughts ruined
the garden held by my soul—
I could see the withered flowers;
I could see the barren land.
All I could do was stare blankly,
While my world was shattering rapidly.

"Why are you so quiet lately?"

The noises are loud.

"But it is silent here."

It's not.
The noises are in me; in my head–
All tangled; all mixed.
I cannot differentiate.
It's getting hard.
I want to stop all this,
But I cannot.
I wish I could escape
From this world's knot.

Life feels like a burden,
I don't think I will be able to bear it.
I'm sorry, but I give up,
I can't feel anything anymore,
I just want to hang up.
I couldn't perform well,
I can just say sorry,
Please don't ask for explanations,
Because I don't have words for it.
I am tired. I want to leave this world,
But destiny is not letting me;
The pain is unbearable.
At times, I want someone to listen,
But the next instant,
I don't want to be approached.
I cannot die, but at least let me hide.
I don't want to face anyone.
I 'cannot' face anyone.
I want nothing, but peace,
But there is not a single place
Where I can peacefully sleep.
The fear is overpowering me,
I hope it turns out to be just a nightmare,
But I know it's real.
The world is just a rat trap
in which I am tangled,
I want to leave it,
I want to be strangled.

She's like the bird escaped from a cage,
She's like the entire ocean in a drop;
She'll realise her own worth soon,
She just needs a chance to hop.
She always embraces others,
She never thought of herself;
She was always doubted,
She lost herself.
She can never be brought back,
She yearns for peace;
She was never at fault,
She is leece.
All the chaos in her mind
Needs to be replaced.
She tried her best,
But was never praised.
She never asked for it,
But it was needed;
Nobody was around her
When she pleaded.
She needed support,
Not mere words;
You thought it an act,
But she was at her worst.
It's an unending story,
There is no other way;
She's just finding a place
To forever lay.

All those years I asked
To shut the voices in my head,
Now, when they are gone,
I feel like I have lost myself.
I realise they were only there
To keep me alive,
Now I am a living corpse,
Hoping to make existence a lie.

In a room full of crowd,
I was still alone
With the crowd in my head.
Sitting in a corner,
I became the wallflower
Which was shrinking
In the trap.

I thought I healed,
But then why did I cry again?
Those memories flashed in front of my eyes,
Why did I feel that sting again?
I thought I had forgotten them,
Did I ever heal then?

She's calm yet storms inside her.
She laughs yet pain behind it.
She never shows who she is,
For she fears the world
which is nothing but an abyss.

She did everything,
But she wasn't good enough.
She doesn't ask anymore "why me?"
Now that she knows it's always her.
She has isolated herself,
in her room;
Little do they know
what those days and nights hold.

My paintbrush,
My canvas,
Strokes of crimson red,
Painting a never-ending mess.
It was hard to survive,
But anyhow I did;
My soul has suffered
more than the art I did.

We talk about the people who stayed,
But what if no one stayed for her?
She was only made to love
and not to be loved.
She gave her everything,
Yet she failed to get what she deserved.

Fake laughs all over,
Screams under the covers.
She acts strong,
Yet she remains alone.
She hides everything so well,
But those walls, those floors know
what secrets she held.

Burdened by the feelings,
I tried to come out of my shell,
But whenever I did,
I faced only hell.
They asked me to speak more,
Unaware that I was battling my own sorrows.
How should I explain them that
Happiness cannot be borrowed?

A sky full of stars,
She stares at which,
Hoping to get a hand of support,
So, she can switch–
To another place.
To another world.
To the place where,
She'll have her own word.
Her choices,
Her regrets,
Her flaws,
Flowed down her cheeks,
As she stared ,
Hoping to get peace.

Drops falling on the ground,
Tears on her cheek;
Drops stopped,
Tears persist.
Drops were there,
When no one was;
She was miserable,
Who knows the cause?
Dark clouds hovering in the night,
Just the way darkness covers her vite.

She cries when happy,
For her heart overflows and spills.
She cries when angry,
For tears help extinguish the flame.
She cries when sick,
For tears heal her wounds.
She cries when sad,
For tears calm the chaos.
She is a sensitive soul,
For she feels to the core.

Mirror, mirror, on the wall,
Where did my confidence fall?
One moment I was having a blast,
The other, their comments did last.
I said I was okay,
But the mirror never lied;
As more as I stared,
I found the lines.
I tried to draw stars around them,
Only to bleed more;
Little did I know,
I couldn't get up anymore.

Why is it always rain
and not a thunderstorm?
Why are there always silent cries
and not the screams and roar?
Why do I have to lock myself
to release my emotions?
Why can you not understand me
from my words and actions?
Yet you expect me to understand you
from your mere reactions.

I can no longer recognise the face on the mirror,
Once believed to be the kindest soul,
The world shaped her into a monster,
And now she regrets it all.
She was harsh upon herself,
Yet there she stands;
Each day, she fights within,
to mask the art, she draws on her hands.

There was magic in her innocent eyes,
She believed her surroundings were magical.
For her, princesses were real,
And the princes were near.
As she grew, she looked for her castle,
But her castle was just four dark walls.
The laughter in the castle was a delusion,
For she always heard the screams and confusion.
Princesses died; princes fall silent,
Her castle crumbled down.
At the end, she was left with
harsh reality as her only remnant.

If I could turn back time,
I would go back to being a teenager—
Console her, hug her
and will tell her to continue;
For there's something big
waiting for her.
Then, I would go to a little girl
who was happy,
who was innocent;
Happily doing a whirl.
Then I would go back to a child
and will erase her presence;
For she has to suffer a lot,
And this is the only way,
She can protect herself.

I am standing still,
The world is in chaos.
Everything around me is moving,
Nowhere to go now
out of this chaos.
I want to go
to some peaceful hill,
Where I can empty myself and scream.
All alone in the dark,
I lay there;
Gazing at the stars,
Everything stayed right there.

I want to escape;
I don't know where I'll go,
But not here.
I want to escape;
I don't know who'll be hurt,
But I will not tolerate myself.
I want to escape;
I don't know what's wrong,
But will find some way,
As I'll escape.

I was silent for a long time.
I faked a smile.
I refused to go out.
I wanted to be alone.
It was not me for a long time
And it went unnoticed by you.
You say you know me,
Then why the change in my behaviour
didn't bother you?

I was never like this.
I hate being me.
All the rage was once love.
All the anxiety was once happiness.
It was never my fault,
Then why blame me?
I try to stay calm,
But it's out of my control.
Still, I'm there for you always,
Even if you are not.

Comforting someone with the words
You wish to hear,
Helping someone because
No one did that for you.
Showing kindness because you know
How it feels to be judged,
But still getting the same which
You wished to never come again.
It is here again, and I wanted to leave.
I did my best yet got the least,
Do I really deserve all this?

Street lamp flicker all night,
Under the rain shower,
Stands a girl, trying to hide—
Hiding from reality,
Hiding from monsters,
Hiding and hiding,
Hiding from this cruel world.
She exists but she doesn't,
No one knows about her.
She's always under her covers.
There she has her own world,
Where she is the happiest,
Where she always runs to
Whenever she is the saddest.

And there I stood staring the same place,
I could find a girl laying her head down.
Tears streaming as if the river's flowing,
Want to be heard, but no one is by her side.
Painting on her arm under sleeve,
So that no one could see her week.
Night passed, tears dried.
Somehow, she lifted her up,
Just to wake up the next day with a (fake) smile.
I smiled remembering her,
How far she has come;
Only I could say is—
She's still trying,
Still trying.

And it felt like
I was losing myself again.
I tried to hold onto it,
But I failed again.
I started from bare minimum,
Thinking I would get
At least what I deserved,
But at the end,
I just lost myself again.

That fake smile–
Was all she could have at the end,
But you,
You never try to look behind it.
She was burning,
She was suffering,
But you,
You just saw that (fake) smile.
And thought she was alright,
Although she was dying,
But you,
You ignored the truth that was always there;
But you,
You never took a chance to care.

She was always the second option,
No one's priority;
She was a mere backup plan,
Always a bin for rant.
She was always kind,
Still left behind;
She thought she was chosen,
But instead she was always an option.

Oh! Is it night again?
There she went lost again.
Maybe in her room,
Under the covers;
Bleeding tears;
Silent cries.

The last tear escaped my eye,
Then my eyes became dry.
I told myself to hang in a little longer,
But I knew it was growing stronger.
Screams faded into the walls,
Cries flew away;
I thought I became more bold,
Yet I failed once more.

Walking and walking,
I reached a land-
Deserted and worn.
I sat on the bench.
As the tears dropped,
I saw a green twig growing.
I vent once,
A leaf grew.
I spoke twice,
A flower bloomed.
Till evening,
That worn land was a whole garden,
Filled with the green of my sorrows.

I see through the sky,
The stars were so silent today.
I see the moon wasn't there.
I could feel how lonely they were.
I was feeling the same.
I started talking to stars.
Today I felt,
I was not alone.
We all were burning,
Just to shine the other day,
And in no second,
We could find ourselves embracing each other.

She is mean yet kind,
She is quiet yet wild.
She is a beautiful contradiction,
Who is fighting the evil and benign.

I was acting at the theatre.
So obsessed with it,
I learnt how to act.
Even when the hall was empty,
I was still acting.
It started to run in my blood,
Emotions within me.
Then one day,
Someone asked me,
“Why are you still acting?”
And that was when I realised,
I forgot how to even express myself,
I became numb that day; once and for all.

I lost myself,
In such a void
That I am forever lost;
No matter how hard I try.
I kept erasing myself,
In the midst of chaos,
And now I have learnt,
It was only my loss.
I gave happiness to everyone,
Only to keep tears for me.
I gave everything to them,
Only to create a void within me.
I lost pieces of my soul,
Gradually and gradually-
Now it's empty,
Just like a cavity.

It was all going good,
Then a sudden wave of sadness
filled inside me.
I seeked that room again,
I seeked those tools again.
I avoided it but failed to.
I wanted to come back,
But I felt dragged by something.
Something inside me stays there always,
Which brings it back every time.
Don't seek me for it,
For it never comes by my will.

Somewhere in this chaos,
I lost myself.
What I want to do is,
Just sit with myself.
I cannot be late,
or I'll lose her.
She is getting separated,
I want to hold her.

She breaks every time,
Still stands again
As if nothing had happened.
She's been a warrior all along,
Smiling, even when everything was broken.
She learnt to stand alone,
Needing company, no more.
She has raised herself so strong,
And now, she will conquer the world.

"Escapism is not good," they say,
But what do I do when everything is slipping away?
I cannot watch it go, nor I can hold it,
Escapism is the only way to make through it.
Every hour, minute and second,
I spend escaping the world.
How does it feel to truly feel?
I guess I have forgotten.
I sit, numb, at night,
Lost in the thoughts.
What went wrong,
When I thought everything was right?

Section 2

The way dusk appears same as dawn,
I wish you would come back to me,
Like you were never gone.
Between dusk and dawn, stars shine,
I remember your face when
You used to whine.
The way moon dips in the night ocean,
I want to dip in you without precaution.
Can you ask dusk and dawn to come together?
You would find no difference;
I wish our souls mingle,
Vanishing the distance.

"How do you keep that charm always?"

Always?
I wish I could tell you the real story,
I wish I could show you the real me,
But I cannot,
I cannot tell you who I am.
Why?
Because I'm afraid,
You'll leave me like others did;
Because I'm afraid,
You won't love me the way you do;
Because I'm afraid,
We'll be strangers with memories again.

"Why didn't you tell?"

I did ,
But you never cared;
Never cared to notice,
Never cared to listen.
Every word was fading away,
I thought you'd notice,
When laughter turned to whispers,
When tears turned to rage,
But–
But you chose to ignore;
Chose to leave,
Chose to abandon.
Still, I had hope,
But the hope vanished
through my fingers like sand.
Did I speak too softly?
Was it easy to turn me away?
Now I stand in silence,
Watching your shadow fleet away.

She was gone in a minute,
You didn't even notice.
She tried to tell,
But she was silenced.
You say you regret that,
But you'll forget her soon too.
She was lonely,
And nobody knew.
She laughed and made you laugh,
Not knowing what was behind her smile.
You, who stated, would love her the most
Also failed to notice.

"You are lying, you are faking."

But have you ever wondered
the way I am changing.

"You are getting mad for no reason."

But have you undergone the things I suffered?
You are questioning my current behaviour,
But did you listen to me when I was vulnerable?
You muted me always
And now you cannot tolerate my loud voice.
You told me to seek you for help,
Then why did you hide at the end?

I thought you would be by my side,
As you promised ;
So, I became an open book to you.
I told you what I feared,
But you did the same to me,
And made a huge pool of my tears.

Shut the voices in my head,
I'm tired of them.
I want to scrap them.
I want to get rid of them.
I don't want to think about it,
Yet you drown me into it.
You promised to hold me,
Yet you were the one to push me.

This was what your sorry felt like—
A glass broken,
Yet put together by band aids.
The more I pour in,
The more it spills out.

She cried and cried,
Until she went numb.
Didn't you see it
or did she never let you see it?
Her dried tears.
Her swollen eyes.
Her messy state.
Her falling apart skies.

I don't think anymore
Anything will get fine,
I have learnt to show
that I am on cloud nine.
Even when my world is falling apart,
I'll be the one to be by your aid;
I know that I'll get alright,
But will never again tell you of my ache.

I remember the rose you gave me,
It was still there—
Dried and worn out,
But still there.
I saw it today,
It had turned black.
I wanted to throw it away,
But there was some beauty that it held.
Memories flooded,
How could you do that?
Tell me so that I can throw it away too,
Just the way you threw away
my love towards you.

They knew something was off,
But they never cared.
She knew that they love,
But never felt that love.
They knew they lack expression,
But never tried to change themselves.
She knew they were there for her,
Yet she went through all by herself.
Their actions were justified,
But her speech wasn't.
They themselves lacked understanding,
Still, she was being nagged standing.

Take my heart,
Take my soul,
Take me as a whole.
Somewhere there,
Somewhere in the universe,
Somewhere in the black hole.
I prayed,
I begged,
I laid.
You saw me,
You knew me,
But you never cared.

There was crowd all over,
Noises were of many;
The voices all over the place,
Everything seemed uncanny.
I found you among all those people,
Thinking you were different,
But you walked away,
Leaving me behind in distress.
How could you even do that?
It was never 'you'.
I thought you were there for me,
But it was all untrue.
All those promises,
All that love,
They all were thrown in the trash;
I thought you would join my shattered pieces,
But I found them more smashed.

Six feet never felt so far,
Are you listening to me?
I hope you are.
Are you here
or stuck between heaven and hell,
or maybe got dissolved
in this world's spell?
There was much more for us
to catch upon,
But you went there alone.

And since then,
I stopped making efforts-
Efforts so that you recognise me,
Efforts to make myself visible.
Why do I have to make an effort every time,
When you don't care?
You are no one to blame me
For my behaviour.
I know I was not like this always,
But did you ever think,
Where did all this come from?

My heart chose you,
Not a good option.
You walked away,
It was predictable.
My heart is torn between,
Allure of freedom and
The embrace of love,
I knew this from the start,
Still, I gave it a chance.
I don't understand why you blame me,
Even though I was the only one,
To put in all the efforts for 'us'.
It was foolish of me to think,
That there existed an 'us'.

She lost her will to live,
He wanted her to stay.
He begged and pleaded,
But she turned away.
She started counting leaves,
Hanging on the wall.
She would be no more,
As the last leaf would fall.
They tumbled down,
Leaf by leaf.
As the last day came near,
The last leaf never left.
She got her will back,
Though she lost him.
His masterpiece remained,
A reason to be reclaimed.

Section 3

Thoughts....
Thoughts....
Thoughts....
Free me from my thoughts.
I am drowning in them.
It's just air around,
Yet it's suffocating till death.

In the quiet of evening,
Shadows stretch and bend.
Everyone rustling back,
The night sets.
Days after days,
Hassle after hassle,
Moon and stars in the sky,
Whispers of dreams begin to blend.

The stars I once believed in,
Don't guide me back home.
Guiding through new places,
They show me the paths to freely roam.
Each way getting to know myself more,
I came a long way,
But there are many lanes left,
Which are calling me along their bay.
I may not see the path clearly,
But I want to reach the end.
Even if the end is never there,
I want to see the infinite blend.

Whole night
Screaming into the pillows
In a dark room-
Just to wake up the next day all fine.
There must really be something,
That changed the inner child
In that span of time.

Having the potential,
Still failing to do it.
Feeling like trash,
I guess I deserved it.
At the end, disappointment is left;
Everything leaving my hand,
Just like the sand.
Lost all the hopes,
Pages are empty.
Floor is painted
In brick red.

Eyes are dried,
They are empty.
Nights are futile,
Turning me up like a bad penny.
No place to survive,
No person to talk;
I have always been by myself,
And now I have learnt to show.

Flowers are meant to wilt,
No matter what you do to conserve them.
People are meant to leave,
No matter what you do to stop them.

Some days are harsh,
Some days are sublime.
May be in another world,
I end up all fine.
Everything was good,
Then why the sudden change?
May be in another world,
I get rid of this rage.

I describe myself as mosaic-
Not clear but still forming pattern,
Blur but still there,
Sharp but soft to the eyes.
Only looking deeper
can help untangle the mystery of mine.

Travelling in the world,
The traveller came back
to his hometown;
Where his soul is attached.
It doesn't feel like home anymore-
Merely a city of labyrinth.
He wandered every lane,
Each depicting an untold tale.
He travelled everywhere,
But couldn't find peace.
He missed those days,
When he was truly free.
He saw his younger self,
Wandering through the town,
Wishing one day he could travel around.
Although his wish came true,
He is not happy.
He wants to go back to his past
And relive those moments,
When he wandered through the streets
Being lost in the magic.

Today white colour spoke to me-
"How does it feel to be thrown away?"
"How does it feel to be thought of as useless?"

For the very first time
I collected all the white coloured pencils
And drew a pattern with them
which gave me all my answers
To the questions which I thought
were never meant to be answered.

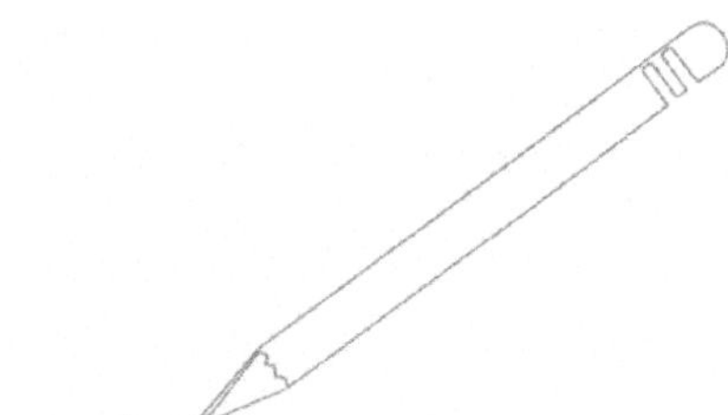

Twinkle, Twinkle little star,
A coward monster you are.
Played me like a toy at my back,
Not had the confidence to front stab.
You remain coward all your life,
Just scaring people out of fright.

Ever felt like a side character in your own story?
Ever been sidelined when you should have been the main character?
It always feels like someone is taking your place.
Now you will say it's just you who isn't trying;
It's just you who is over exaggerating.
"Not trying" "Over exaggerating" Really?
I have never prioritised myself;
Always thought about others,
And now, for once, when I thought of myself,
I became selfish;
Even when I felt lost,
Even when I got sidelined.

If I ever met my younger self,
I'll tell her to stop being so harsh on herself.
I'll tell her to enjoy the time.
I may not tell her the reality.
She is so innocent.
I may not scare her-
Of the people.
Of the devils.
Of the world.

People come and go,
Whom to trust and whom to let go?
In a room full of masks,
I kept my real face.
That was the day I realised-
The world is full of knots,
So tight, they hurt,
So many, they can't be undone.

Wind slipped through my window,
Whispering the secrets of nature,
Held with tender love;
Bringing back the memories of last autumn.
Carrying leaves as their messengers,
They go on a long way ahead,
With all the memories and affection,
With every gentle breath.

Some wants to go in past,
Some in future.
But if you ask me,
I just want to be here.
But my thoughts ruined me,
They took me to the past.
They took me to the future.
I wanted to take a halt here,
But my thoughts....

Everything is illusional,
Yet, mosaic.
Minds are messed up,
Don't know how to act.
Everything is still,
Yet moving.
Echoes in the mind,
Chasing, never losing.

Somewhere in the air,
Somewhere in my mind,
Lost between the woods,
Lost somewhere in the line.
Not sure where I am;
Maybe in the whispers of wind,
Maybe in abodes of evil.
I'm trying to find myself,
Or maybe I lost my will.

In the silence between words,
I found the noises of thoughts.
In the untangled strings of stillness,
I found the tangled net of chaos.

Everything was messy,
So, I took out the page.
The page told me a different story.
My own thoughts were strangled,
The page was empty.
I realised it wasn't only me,
But the world that was silent;
And that paradox
was never meant to be broken.

My heart is not intact,
But the pieces still work.
Hope lingers in between,
It's not the same, but it endures.

"It must feel so good to be a writer."

No, it doesn't.
Writers are the cursed souls-
Cursed to feel deeply,
Cursed to feel overly,
Cursed to not be numb,
Cursed to be the destruction.

Bleeding on paper,
With black ink.
Internal haemorrhage,
With crimson red tint.

A heart never breaks.
Have you ever heard of it?
It withers,
Withers until it fades.
It traps your soul inside
And shrink with time.
The chest pain is the
Soul's mournful cry.
Heart never breaks,
It merely withers away.

Stuck in the maze,
Stuck in the asylum,
Not able to find a way back home.
Hidden doors, magic lanes,
Not sure where the obstacles are born.
One door leads to other,
But none to the exit.
I'm tired of this labyrinth,
But I simply cannot quit.

The pain that you feel,
When the tears are on the brink,
But you have to act all fine.
You hide it so well
Behind your sweet smile.

There was an ocean,
Full of emotions.
Words lay at the depths,
Smile on the surface.
Surface was silent,
A hurricane at the depth.
It was meant to stay silent,
For it was too raw to reveal-
The feeling of being concealed.

She is here again.
I wonder how she was today.
Pouring her emotions on my pages,
I absorb her tears.
I wish I could tell her,
I'll always be here.
She can find comfort in my embrace,
In every word, I hold her grace.
-Her Diary

“Why do you write?”

My tears are dried, my soul shattered.
What should I do
When my heart is in vain?
I try and try,
And still trying.
But poetry is the only one
Which gives me hope-
That I am not alone in this cave.

Death has never scared me.
What has scared me the most is-
Can't make up till death.
When you failed what scared you the most,
Everything inside dies.
That's how a poet's soul is made.

Always the writer, never the muse,
Were you only mine to lose?
Always the listener, never been heard,
Yet always there, whenever you are struck.
Always making efforts, never seen them return,
Still always there whenever you yearn.
Always the poet, never the poem,
In my thoughts, you always roam.
It was late for me to understand that I was
Always to love, but never been loved.

I wish I could hold the time;
Adoring the sunset,
With pure love and devotion.
The place where I forget all my fears,
My pain;
The time which gives me peace.
I bid a goodbye to the sun,
Wishing for the moon,
To shine with its full potential;
And the thought just struck to my mind-
Every good thing ends,
Just to be more beautiful the next day.

Somewhere is light,
Somewhere a shadow.
Both are inseparable,
Winding like a meadow.
Still darkness engulfed me,
Held me into its embrace.
It was out of my control,
I just surrendered.
I know that was not a good move,
But still I did.
I am tired from everything,
I want to quit.

Chaos turned into calm,
When I wrote it on pages.
Pages turned red,
When I bled with a pen.
The oceans turned down,
When everything went black.
It was deepness down there,
Where she'll forever rest.

Poetry came to me very early,
In a very different way.
The way it never went;
It embraced me into its words.
Its warmth was more than anything to me,
The only way where I could express myself freely.
I wonder sometimes if I would have never crossed paths with it,
How dry my life would have been?

It's a big accomplishment,
To just survive the day.
It's a big accomplishment,
To carry it so well,
Even when it's heavy.
It's a big accomplishment,
To smile, even when you're tired.
You survived today.
You carried it so well today.
You smiled today.
You accomplished it today.
I'm proud of you.